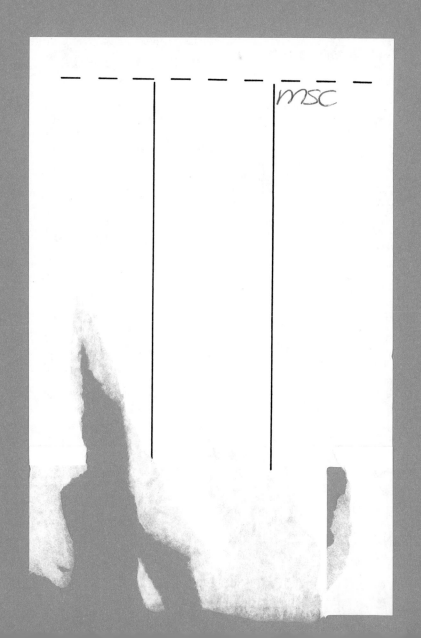

msc

THE TANGLEWEED

TROLL

Cliff Wright

LONDON • VICTOR GOLLANCZ • 1993

Beyond the garden gate
my friends called me to play,

but Daddy said I couldn't go
because of all the wizards

and giants
and pirates
out there,
and the Tangleweed Troll
who'd take me home for supper
if I stepped in the woods.

But I said,
"Daddy, maybe you're a troll,"
and he just smiled and said,
"Jenny, don't let me see you
go outside the garden gate,"

and so he never looked
when I did.

Perhaps I heard a wily wizard call,
"I wonder where can Jenny be?"

"Are you up there . . .

scampering with the squirrels?"

"No! I'm down here,

tracking the Tangleweed Troll."

Perhaps I heard a jumbled giant roar,
"Wherever can that Jenny be?"

"Are you over there . . .

romping with the rabbits?"

"No! I'm under here,

teasing the
Tangleweed
Troll."

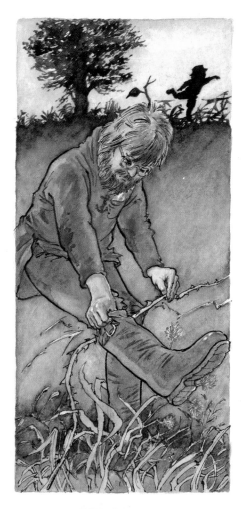

Perhaps I heard a pesky pirate shout,
"Now where on earth can Jenny be?"

"Are you in there . . .

frolicking with the fishes?"

"No! I'm out here,

tricking the Tangleweed Troll."

But suddenly
my happy game was through,
as all my secret friends
deserted me.

Perhaps they'd heard . . .

the stamping, trampling tread   of *my* Tangleweed Troll

who'd come to take me home